Exceptionally Weird

Written by:
Raevyn Sarai

Publication information

PUBLISHER'S NOTE:
Any references or similarities to actual events, entities, real people, living or dead, or to real locales are intended to give the novel a sense of reality. Any similarity in other names, characters, entities, places, and incidents is entirely coincidental. All rights reserved, including the right of reproduction in whole or part in any form.

ISBN:

Library of Congress Control Number: 2017948405

Copyright: 2017

Exceptionally Weird
ISBN 13: 978-0-9991590-2-6
Cover Design: Junnita Jackson
Author: Raevyn Sarai
Published by:
Legacy Publishing Group

Acknowledgements

I thank God for allowing me to be brave enough to write this book.

I want to thank my Pastor, Aunt Shele and Uncle Damion Evans for always coming to see me when I was sick and always asking about me and praying for me when I am not at church.

My Mom-Mom and Pop-Pop, Diane and Robert Williams, I love you guys so much. Thank you for being there for my mother and sister when no one else was.

Aunt Tone I love you.

My sister Tryniti aka Tryn.Bynn, although we are not the same I love you and I am happy you are my sister.

Vianca Black, I love you and thank you for caring for me.

Kani, Karter and Kaiden love you! Oh you too Khalil.

My Williams family love you.

Aunt Tiff

My God-Mother Monique Hills

Dareyonna and Dai-Dai I can't leave y'all out.

My cousins Jon Hall, love you big head, Nayda, Melo, Jayda and Jaylyn

My Uncle John, Aunt Erica, Nylah, Laylah and Gabby.

My Heaven Touched Outreach Family

Last but not least my mommy, Katchan "K.D. Harris" Reid. I remember when I use to hate K.D. Harris, for making us move to

Maryland. I love you and thank you for passing on your gift of writing to me!

If I forgot anyone. I still love you!

Dedication

Polly "MA" Williams
My great-grandma
I still remember our talks…S.I.P

*"If you're always trying to be normal, you will never know how amazing you can be."~ **Maya Angelou***

Table of Contents

My Thoughts...

- *I don't have problems*

- *I don't hate myself*

- *I have friends*

- *I take care of myself*

- *I get good grades*

- *I do what I'm told or expected to do*

- *I'd rather be alone*

- *Why am I never happy?*

- *Why do I fake my smile?*

- *Why do I always have to please everyone?*

- *Why do I feel depressed?*

When will it ever STOP?
Raevyn's Mental

S ometimes I feel like I need to rant. I need to express my feelings to someone who cares enough to listen. I've had counselors in the past-eight to be exact. There was no success. I guess I could admit that the failed sessions were partially my fault, however they were also to blame. Before you judge me let me explain my reasoning.

I've been in some form of counseling since I was 11 years old. I will tell you how I got there in a minute. First, let me set up the scene.

Picture this…I'm 11 years old, put in a huge room with fifteen children with some sort of "mental" issue. This is my first time in this type of environment. My mother is home and I can't go home. Yet, I'm expected to spill out my problems to a group of strangers. Not happening-no way. When I don't respond the way that they think I should, I am then sent to the on-site psychiatrist. I'm thinking that this is my chance to tell someone why I did what I did to get here. The doctor will listen to me-this is what he is paid to do...right? Wrong! Instead of listening to me, he put me on pills. Pills...were so not the answer to my dilemmas.

I was always quiet. My family talks about how I didn't talk until I was four years old. They were exaggerating of course, I could talk, I chose not to. I remember my mother took my older sister and I to a private school for testing. I was three at the time and my sister was seven. She wanted my sister to get in badly. She found out that there was a pre-school program and decided that she wanted me to go as well.

I remember being in a big classroom with other children; something that I was not use to at all. There was a lady talking to me asking me to count blocks, identify colors and a whole lot of other things, which I knew how to do. I didn't respond to any of it. After a few hours, she finally gave up. She sent me to play with the other kids. I wouldn't budge. I sat at the table by myself not talking to anyone the rest of the day. I saw my mother coming towards the door and I blurted out, "My sister got hit by a car." I was calm when I said it. The women turned towards me with a strange look on her face. She was surprised that I could talk. That was the first thing I had said out of my mouth that entire day.

When my mother came in the room, the lady told her that she didn't think I was fit for the program. She actually told my mother that she thought I was traumatized from my sister's accident and that I may need help to deal with it. That didn't sit well with my mom. She snapped all the way home. My sister, Tryn thought it was funny that I didn't talk during the interview. That made my mom angrier. She said something that would be very familiar to my ears in my later years, "Rae why would you say that! People are going to think you are *weird*!"

She told her best friend what happened. Apparently, the advice she gave my mother was to send me to daycare. I thought that was dumb because my mother owned her own daycare center that I was sometimes apart of…when I felt like being bothered. The daycare was attached to our house. I stayed in my room most of the time, by choice. My mother followed her friend's advice and put me in two different pre-schools.

13

The same thing happened. I didn't respond to anything. Eventually she got tired of wasting her money and let me stay home with her.

I guess you can say that is where my *introvert-ness* started. When it was time for me to go to school things didn't change. I kept to myself. I didn't make friends in my early years of school. That's enough about me. You are about to read a story about a girl, close to my age who I have a lot in common with. I'm not going to bore you with my story. Let me introduce you to Ava Morgan…

1

I take care of myself...

"I'm wide awake...yeah, I was in the dark, I was falling hard...with an open heart...I'm wide awake...How did I read the stars so wrong..." I sang along with Katy Perry, as I headed down the stairs to the kitchen to consume the most important meal of the day, breakfast. I entered the kitchen humming and bopping my head to the music that blared through my headphones.

Unlike the families you see on television, my father wasn't sitting at the forefront of the table drinking coffee with the latest Forbes or Black Enterprise magazine in front of his face, munching on a slice of slightly burnt toast with his briefcase close to his side. My mother wasn't at the stove scrambling eggs, frying bacon while flipping perfectly round golden pancakes as my siblings sat around the table smiling and eager to start their school day. There was no aroma of sticky sweet maple syrup in the air. That's not how it worked in my house. My father, lived with his son in lower Delaware along with his girlfriend who couldn't stand the sight of me.

My mom was already on I-95 South headed to her job. My sisters, well the oldest one was still in the bed sleep recovering from a long night of a crying newborn while the other was talking loud from the living room on Facetime with her "best" discussing who she was going to have to *check*-curse out for being

Joe-fake. I went to the cabinet to retrieve my daily brown sugar *Pop Tart*, the very thing that my mom continued to swear she was going to stop buying because she read somewhere on Facebook that it causes Cancer. I opened the fridge and grabbed a *Gatorade* and sat at the table to eat.

As soon as I opened my Pop Tart my sister walks in the kitchen, "Girl! What do you have on! Look at your hair!"

I took a deep breath and braced myself for the insults and negativity that was about to be directed towards me.

"Stand up!" She ordered. I ignored her and kept eating like I always did. "See this is what I be talking about! Why are you wearing that! It's your first day at this school and you going up in there looking all weird! Like really

17

Ava, you're thirteen why are you still wearing stuff from *Justice*. You're too big for that! Why do you keep getting these straight back braids? You look like a dyke!"

I sighed. "I don't see anything wrong with what I have on. I have on a shirt and tights. You wear shirts and tights. A lot of girls wear braids." I replied calmly. I knew if I gave her attitude it would have escalated and I wasn't in the mood for it.

She tossed her 30-inch weave to the side and frowned her face. "What girl? I wear yoga pants that are from PINK my shirt is from PINK. I don't have Justice going down the side of my leg. I don't wear cornrows straight back. I can see if you had on earrings or something. Put on some lip gloss! You are in the 8th grade Ava. No one wears *Justice* or straight backs with no style." She flipped the camera of her iPhone pointing it in my direction. "Look at what she got on "best" Tell her she is going to get flamed-teased! Don't she look like a ni**a! Look at her feet, she's wearing freaking Timberlands! She could have at least thrown on her UGG Boots or Converse." Her best friend, Nikki laughed and said, "She looks alright leave her alone, Kimmie."

My sister sucked her teeth, grabbed her Michael Kors bag and headed to the door, "You so Joe, best! I love my little sister but she don't care about how she looks. She doesn't take care of herself, she is so weird! She busses me with that!" Then she was gone.

There was a part of me that was bothered by what she said. *I do take care of myself...* I heard it so much that I had become numb. I didn't feel anything. It went in through my ears and took a spot in the depth of my soul with the rest of the hurtful, negative feelings I harbored. I was used to it.

I was the youngest child from my mother. My father had other children but I believe there was one more after me. I wasn't sure because I didn't really keep up with them. My mother's oldest child Liv, was twenty-one years old. She had gotten pregnant during her sophomore year in college. She had her daughter, Amya two months ago and moved back home.

Kimberly aka Kimmie was my seventeen-year-old sister. Unlike Liv and me, she was straight action. There was never a dull moment with her around. She had to be the center of attention at all times which lead her to stay in trouble a lot. Most of my mother's free time was spent advocating for her. She knew that Kimmie would be wrong most of the time, but she fought for her, she fought for us all. Without our fathers in the picture and having a small family she figured we were all we had.

A Moment to Relate

Like my friend Ava, I'm sure you too may have been criticized for the music you listened to, the way you wear your hair or style of dressing. Think about a time of when someone made a negative comment about your appearance. What happened?

_____

_____

_____

_____

_____

_____

_____

_____

Use 3 Words to describe the way it made you feel?

- _____

- _____

- _____

Remember, we all experience negative feelings. We just shouldn't hold them in or dwell on them. If we are offended by someone we don't have to lash out and be rude to tell them how we feel. Now go back and read what you wrote and write a positive response.

_____

_____

_____

_____

_____

_____

_____

_____

_____

_____

_____

_____

It's ok not to look like everyone else…if we did the world would be boring.

2

I don't hate myself...

It was a few weeks before my birthday and the third month I had been attending my new school. For the most part, it was ok. I went to my classes, lunch and went home. I didn't participate in any extracurricular activities. I loved to dance, I had been on dance teams in the past and I praised danced at my church-sometimes. I met a few girls who I was comfortable enough with to consider them my friends. That was something new because I never really had friends besides, Yonna and Devan who were more like cousins than friends. I spent most of my time alone in my room, on my phone, watching *Dance Moms* and *So You think you can dance* re-runs.

This particular Friday night, my mother happened to come in my room. There was a look of concern on her face. I was used to seeing her with that expression, however usually it was directed towards my sisters. They were the ones with issues not me. I watched her sit on my bed through the corner of my eye as I continued to text on my phone.

"Ava, do you like yourself?" she asked.
I continued texting and nodded my head, "yeah". She inhaled deeply then exhaled. That's when I noticed she had her phone in her hand.

"I just got off the phone with your dad…"

"I don't have a dad." I said as I continued to text.

"Don't say that. That's still your dad and you have to respect him. The bible says you have to honor your mother and father no matter what. He has to answer for his wrong doings. Don't wear his issues."

Her tone changed up. She was in her feelings. She always got a little heated when I said something negative about my dad. My sisters could call their dad everything in the book. She would give them the same speech but there was no emotion behind it because we knew she couldn't stand him either but that wasn't the case with my dad. It made me mad because he was no different. He chose that woman instead of being a father to me.

"Your dad loves you Ava, things are just crazy right now. Pray for him. It will get better."

I shook my head not wanting to have anything to do with the conversation or him.

27

"What did he say?" I asked, so we could get this over with.

"He wanted to know why you had skinny white girls up as your profile picture on your Facebook page. I told him that these are the girls you follow from that dance show but he thinks it may be more than that."

Now I was annoyed.

"More like what!"

"Like you don't like yourself because you are dark skin and not skinny. You know it's nothing wrong with having a dark complexion. You are pretty. You have nice smooth chocolate skin. You don't have to be pale and paper thin to be considered cute. You do know that right?"

Before I could answer Kimmie comes flaunting herself through the door.

"She don't like herself. You should see her Instagram she has all these fake pages acting like she's these girls. They are all *white* too!"

"They are called fan pages!" I got up from my bed to leave the room. I didn't want to be around them anymore. When I walked by Kimmie she snatched my phone out of my hand. I tried to get it back but she was quick and too tall for me to get it from her. She ran over to my mom and started to scroll through the phone.

"Give me my phone!" I shouted.

My mom's face hardened when she looked through the phone.

I went over to them and reached for my phone and my mom snapped.

"I pay for this phone! Back up!" She rolled her eyes and they both invaded my privacy. I wanted to cry and scream but I held it in. It wasn't fair how I was being treated. She never went through my sister's phone. She paid for her bill too. After she was done she and Kimmie both looked at me in disgust.

"Do you have any *real* friends Ava?" My mother's tone softened.

I didn't respond. I did what I would always do when confronted about things I didn't want to discuss…I would shut completely down.

"No! She don't got no friends. These people don't even know what she really looks like!"

"Shut up, Kimmie!" my mom said.

"Are you okay Ava? You know this is not normal, right?" she said.

"She's weird! I told you that she is WEIRD! You keep babying her up and letting her listen to that white stuff. She thinks she is one of them! She is going to end up being one of those EMO people wearing all black. You're not gonna be satisfied until she tries to kill the entire house. I swear if she tries that crazy ish with me we going to be mixxin'-fighting."

My mother was fed up. "Get the…I swear you about to make me snap! Shut up! That's your sister she is not weird! Just confused."

Kimmie stormed out the room saying things under her breath. Now I'm alone with my mother. We both have thoughts racing through our mind. Hers are mostly likely of concern. Mine are of resentment for being misunderstood, violated and then there is anger.   Anger at my so called father for all of a sudden being concerned of what *my* social media profile picture looked like. What about my school pictures? Did he even ask for one? Why didn't he ask me himself, he had my cell phone number, he could have come and asked me face to face. I'm sure my mother would not have had a problem giving him our address. He probably already knew where we lived anyway.

I also had resentment, resentment towards my sister for always judging me, and coaxing my mother into violating me to invade my privacy. She never went through my sister's phone or questioned them about their social media pages. Why did they always pick on me? Why do I have to please everyone?

People always say how it's ok to be different. You should be yourself. It's all good if they think what you are doing is cool. As soon as you do something they don't like, or misunderstand you're considered *weird* or *dumb*. I was starting to believe that there was no such thing as normal. How can you do normal things if everyone's definition of "normal" is so different? No one on this planet does everything the same way, if that was the case then I guess we all should be labeled *weird*.

A Moment to Relate

How many of you feel like you are misunderstood? If you could see me, you would see that I am raising my hand. There is a saying, "What's understood doesn't have to be explained…" Well this is my version, "What you don't understand is not my issue…it's yours."

I don't think anyone one has to have an explanation for who they are? Or what they like? I don't like fish, should I have to explain why, because you don't understand why I don't like it? The answer is simple…NO! Simply because I relate to another culture means I hate the skin I'm in? NO! Just because you don't hear me on the phone talking to others, I don't hang out or bring people home, does that mean that I am friendless…Absolutely NOT!

My mother told me that people fear what they don't understand. They automatically look at it as if it is not normal. Like church for instance, I go to a church where people shout (dance around because the Holy Spirit hit them) they speak in tongues, (it sounds weird to those who don't understand it) and some people are able to give prophesy. I have friends who don't understand that at all. Some even think that it's like voodoo or something. I didn't think nothing of it because I have always gone to churches like this. I have even experienced God/Holy Spirit telling me somethings.

Think about a time when you were misunderstood by your parents. How did it make you feel?

- _____

- _____

- _____

What do you wish you could talk openly your parents about?

_____

_____

_____

_____

_____

_____

_____

_____

_____

_____

_____

_____

No matter how we feel about our parents at times, we still have to respect them…even if they don't do right by us. I believe my God will handle them.

3

I'd rather be alone...

Christmas break has arrived. Everything at home is great for the most part. This will be my nieces first Christmas and everyone is excited, including Kimmie who tends to be in great spirits around the holiday. Everyone knows she's super excited because her 18th birthday is just around the corner. I found it to be a bitter sweet situation because although she gets on my nerves most of the time. I know she loves me and I love her. I would miss her if she moved out. She claimed she was leaving as soon as she turned eighteen all the time.

It's Christmas Eve and my mother was generous enough to allow Kimmie to take the car so we could go to a party.

Partying wasn't really my thing-that was a Kimmie thing. The only reason I went was because Yonna and Devan were going and the only way my mother was giving up the keys was if I went. She knew if things went left, I would call her immediately. Yes, I was labeled the snitch but I was okay with it. We arrived at the American Legion Lodge where the teen party was held. Kimmie took her time getting out the car, she had to make sure her hair and make-up was on point. She was wearing her hair in long box braids that hung passed her butt. Kimmie was at least 5 foot 8 inches. She was tall, with a thick build. Her stomach was flat, it was her hips and thighs that got the attention of boys and some grown men. She wore clothes that showed how "bad" her body was leaving a lot of girls who had "too much" or "not as much" assets upset.

I was the complete opposite. I stood 5 feet even and was on the chunky side. I wasn't fat but I was far from skinny. It was weird because during the summer Yonna and I were the same size. Most people thought we were twins. It seemed as my pounds packed on and hers disappeared.

I never paid attention to it until that night. We were both wearing black lace shorts and crop tops that we brought off the clearance rack at none of other than *Justice*. Kimmie was wearing a black pencil skirt and a black crop top with a fringed pair of "Thot" boots.

Devan was the only one dressed appropriately for December weather. I guess he didn't need to dress a certain way because he was a guy. Needless to say, I was uncomfortable with my outfit. If it were up to me I would have worn jeans and a hoodie.

Once we were inside we were in complete darkness. The place was jammed packed with sweaty teenagers dancing or should I say *swagging* each other. Kimmie came over to Yonna and me and laid down her rules, "Y'all stay with each other at all times. If you need me, hit my phone. If a chick tries to talk crazy let me know!" Then she disappeared into the crowd. It wasn't long before some boys tried to dance with us. Yonna had no problem with the attention. I loved to dance but I wasn't really trying to get *swagged*. I decided not to be "weird" as Kimmie would say and started to throw it back so the guy could swag me. I had to admit after a while I had really started to get into it. I danced to a few more songs before I heard my sister's voice,

"Yup, Ava I see you! Aye...Aye...Aye!" She started dancing next to me. When the song was over the guy who was dancing with me acted like he was trying to do a little more than dance.

"Yo, chill." Kimmie said pushing him away. "That's my lil sis, she's thirteen. I know you ain't trying to catch a charge or these hands." She threatened him. He backed away holding his hands in the air apologizing. Apparently, he was eighteen years old. I thought age limit for the party was cut off at seventeen. I felt weird after that. There was no way he thought I was older. I looked like a little girl still. I was hot and pretty much over the party after that so I went outside and sat on the steps. It was only 10:30 p.m. and the party wasn't over until midnight. We had to leave a half hour before "let out" because that's when the fights would occur.

As I sat outside in the cold. I watched groups of people go in and out of the party. Most were going outside to smoke weed in their cars, while a few went around the side of the building to mess around. I couldn't believe what I was seeing. I mean, I knew that people did these type of things but some of the kids were my age and they were having sex outside with high school aged boys and girls. Just about every girl was now a lesbian or bisexual. I was taught that it was wrong to be gay that's why I hated it when people would say I was a dyke. I had nothing against people who were like that but that wasn't my life and I am not the one who was going to have to answer to God about it.

While I was sitting on the steps I saw a girl from my school named Zina. She was smoking a blunt alone under a tree. Zina was in the 8th grade like me but she hadn't been to school in weeks. There were rumors around school that she was pregnant by her stepfather. She didn't look pregnant to me, she was skinny as a rail. When she finished smoking she came over to me, "You're *KimK302's* sister right?" She asked referring to my sisters Instagram name.

"My name is Ava, but yeah that's my sister." She laughed a slow goofy laugh.

"I know what your name is. I just didn't know that she was your sister. I know it *has* to be hard having her as a sister. I mean, she's so popular and everyone *loves* her. She's like Delaware famous and you're..." I got up to walk away from her. She grabbed my arm. "My bad

Ava. It's that you guys are so different. I know that living in her shadow is a problem."

"I don't live in her shadow. We are two different people. She likes to be seen and I don't. I'd rather be alone."

"I know what you mean. I don't like being around people too much either. I know you probably heard all types of rumors about why I am not in school. The truth is, I had too many problems at home so I couldn't focus. I would come to school angry. Instead of taking my anger out on others, I isolated myself. It got so bad that they tried to send me to one of those mental centers. They thought I was suicidal."

"Were you...I mean did you want to kill yourself?" I interrupted her. While she was talking I thought back to how she behaved when she was in school. She didn't hang with anyone. She always sat by herself at lunch and she never walked in the hallways with anyone. She was a loner and she did look sad all the time.

She shrugged her shoulder. "I thought about it. I cut myself a few times." She turned on the light on her phone to show me the red scars from the self-inflicted cuts on her arm." Instead of cringing from the sight of them, I became more curious.

"Did it hurt…does it hurt?" She shrugged her shoulders again. "No not really…I think it made me feel better. I can't really explain it. But there was really no use to going through with it. I was already dead to everyone anyway. No one cared about me. They never spoke to me, they just ignored me like I wasn't even there.

"So why did you come to this party? I thought you liked being alone?" I asked.

She laughed again. "This was the only way I could actually be alone. I know it sounds complicated. I stay with my grandma now and she has my aunt living with her along with three little crumb snatchers. They want me to be more social so I heard about this party and said I wanted to go. My aunt dropped me off and watched me go in. As soon as she pulled off, I left and went to my chill spot under that tree indulging in my herbal refreshments." A smile spreads across her thin face.

"Herbal refreshments?" I rolled my eyes and gave her a half smile. "I never heard it referred to as an herbal refreshment. Loud, Gas, Reggie and Chow is what they call it.

"I live with my dad's side of the family. My aunt is bougie! That is what she calls it. She tries to keep it classy." We both laughed. "You should try it. It takes the anger away."

"No, I don't do drugs. Besides I can't get angry if I stay to myself."

A Moment to Relate

Zina isolated herself from people because she felt that she would be rejected. I isolated myself because I was afraid that if I would be my true self and try to make friends or talk to my family members I would get pushed away. I thought if I stayed to myself I wouldn't have to worry about rejection. I never understood how people like my sister could make friends so easily and it was so hard for me.

When you isolate yourself, you lose connection with the outside world. It didn't bother me when I was alone but it bothered everyone around me. They didn't think it was normal that I wanted to be left alone. I learned that when I isolated myself I eventually stopped caring about everything. I didn't care how I

49

looked, I didn't bathe as much. I quit dancing which was something I loved to do. I didn't want to go to church or any other events. I wanted to be alone.

Isolation can cause paranoia as well. I thought everyone was against me. I thought I saw people peeking in on me in the room, even though I knew I was in the house alone. I tricked myself into isolation because I was afraid of what people would think of me. I didn't think it was a big deal. I wasn't bothering anyone so no one should bother me. I didn't realize that I was slowly driving myself insane...for nothing. This was all in my head because I was afraid of rejection.

Ecclesiastes 4:12

Though one may be overpowered, two can defend themselves. A cord of three is not quickly broken.

It's not good to be alone. No matter how isolated from the world you want to be, it's bad. Remember you don't need a bunch of friends. It can be you, one other and God!

Think of a time when you may have isolated yourself. Write down what caused you to isolate.

_____

_____

_____

_____

_____

_____

_____

_____

_____

_____

Do you feel like you're are being rejected? If so why.

_____

_____

_____

_____

_____

_____

_____

_____

List 4 Great things about yourself that others should know.

- _____

- _____

- _____

• _____

Zina talked about cutting herself to make herself feel better. There are many teens who believe that self-inflicting pain on themselves soothes their stress. There are many ways that they harm themselves:

- Cutting (scratching or using razor blades)

- Pulling out their hair

- Picking their skin/face

- Punching/hitting their self

I picked at my face when I felt anxious, or to release bad feelings I was having. My mother would constantly tell me to stop it. I would tell her that I was itching from acne. She of course knew I was lying. She knew it was anxiety causing me to do this. So whenever she saw me do this she would engage me in some type of activity or conversation to take my mind off of whatever I was thinking or worrying about.

If you ever have the urge to self-injure, or if you already do it, talk to someone you trust. Someone who can help you cope with your bad feelings like, your mentor, older sibling, cousin, pastor or any adult that you trust including your parent.

If you ever caused self-injury to yourself think about why you did.

_____

_____

_____

_____

_____

_____

_____

_____

_____

_____

_____

_____

_____

List things you can do when you feel Stressed, Anxious or Upset instead of self-harming.

- _____

- _____

- _____

- _____

- _____

Who can you talk to when you are feeling down?

_____

_____

_____

_____

_____

_____

_____

_____

_____

4

Why do I feel depressed?

Winter break was officially over. It was time for me to return to school. I kept in touch with Zina over the break and I learned a lot about her. She did have a lot of issues. Her parents were drug addicts and often fought in front of her and her siblings. Sometimes she wouldn't even have anything to eat, or clean clothes because they spent all of their money on drugs. Zina was bullied and teased about the way she looked and sometimes smelled when she came to school. This was the reason why she stopped coming. She was only fourteen, which meant she couldn't drop out of school. So, she was sent to the Rockford Center's Day Program because of the cutting. Once she was done with that she would be on homebound, which meant the teacher would come to her home to teach her.

I wish I was able to go to school from home. During the break, the few girls that I considered friends kind of turned on me when I told them I was now friends with Zina. My one friend, Anna had the nerve to ask me was I now a lesbian, because rumor had it that Zina was not only pregnant but a lesbian as well. The lesbian part was true, Zina admitted to liking girls, but that wasn't my problem and I wasn't going to stop being friends with her because of it.

That first week back was hell. I was asked a thousand questions about Zina's personal life. No one asked what I got for Christmas or what I did over the break, they just wanted the juice-gossip on Zina. The same girl that they ignored when she was actually a student at the school. I didn't give too many details just a few to keep them off my back. Once they found out none of the rumors were true it was back to cracking jokes and playing around. It seemed as if everything was fine, but in my mind, I was screaming for help! What kind of help... I wasn't sure of. I just knew that there was something wrong and I hid it by smiling like everything was great.

Things at home didn't change much either, my mother was still trying to get me to visit my dad's family in hopes I would get a connection with him. I told her countless times, that I wasn't interested. Don't get me wrong, I loved my mom-mom and pop-pop, but spending time with them was not going to bring my dad to see me. He didn't care. Last winter I was in the hospital for an entire week and he never showed up. My Uncle and Grandparents did, but not my dad. He did call, but that was nothing. I was too sick to talk on the phone.

I was starting to gain more weight. I didn't care but my mother did. She would watch me as I put food on my plate, or yell at me when I spent my allowance on a cheesesteak instead of going to the mall to buy something else other than food.

One Sunday after church service everyone was sitting around talking, this one lady named, Ms. May that came to the church often would always compliment me on my smile or the way I praise danced. This day she called me over and said, "Ava, I almost didn't know that was you! You picked up *sooo* much weight!" Immediately the smile disappeared from my face. I could feel the tears stinging in my eyes.

I hurried out the church in embarrassment. I was starting to hate being around people. They would say anything not caring how anyone else felt. It was bad enough looking in the mirror and seeing what you were becoming but to hear it from someone else who is not family hurt to the core.

After that day things changed for the worse. I couldn't fall asleep at night. By the time I did fall asleep it was time to get ready for school. Somedays I would act like I was going and miss the bus on purpose. I knew my mother was at work so I would leave the back door unlocked to go back home and sleep and of course eat. I was no longer happy. I faked smiles and kept my grades up so my mother wouldn't realize what was happening. That didn't last long. Things went from bad to worse in a blink of an eye.

A Moment to Reflect

Some people can put on a smile for you, laugh and joke around like everything is ok. Except, it's not ok. They're screaming on the inside for someone to understand their pain. They want someone to show that they care and ask, "What is wrong?"

"What can I do to help you?"

I would cry at night, hoping, praying and waiting asking God for things to get better. I was mentally and physically breaking down.

You'd never know what is going on with someone unless you ask.

My mother would ask me, and I wouldn't have an explanation, because I had no idea what was wrong with me. I just knew I felt empty.

Have you ever felt depressed? If so explain.

_____

_____

_____

_____

_____

_____

_____

_____

_____

_____

Signs of Depression

- Sadness or hopelessness.
- Irritability, anger, or hostility.
- Tearfulness or frequent crying.
- Withdrawal from friends and family.
- Loss of interest in activities.
- Poor school performance.
- Changes in eating and sleeping habits.

Which symptoms of depression have you encountered?

- _____

- _____

- _____

- _____

It's hard for people to talk about their feelings. They may feel like no one will understand them. Or sometimes they may feel if they talk to certain people they will not get the response they are looking for. I know when I would talk to my mom, depending on the mood she was in, I would get a ghetto, churchy, or a psychological answer. So, most of the time I didn't go to her. She was too deep and all over the place.

Sometimes people take what we say the wrong way and get offended when you don't agree with their advice. People may not look at their situation the same or have the same point of view as others; which is fine because it is in fact *their* point of view or opinion.

I learned that sometimes it's best to sit back for a moment and figure out a situation for myself. I get a journal and write out the pros vs the cons. I then focus on the positive more than the negative.

It is important to think positive. Here are a few great positive Affirmations to say when you are feeling down; when you wake up or before you go to bed at night!

- The more I like myself, the more others will like me.

- I have people who care about me and will help me if I need it.

- I will ask for help if I need it.

- My dreams are achievable.

- The people who may judge me are the people who are most afraid of being judged.

- In 5 years, it is not going to matter what I wore today.

- I do not need drugs or alcohol to have fun.

- I love myself unconditionally.

- I am not lost, I'm still creating myself.

- I begin my day by affirming the positive and end my day with gratitude.

- I see the beauty in stopping to appreciate my blessings.

- I am happy. Who else am I trying to please?

- I love and respect my family for all they do for me.

- **I am completely unique and therefore, there are no rules to what I am and am not!**

  Embrace your Uniqueness!

Use these pages to add some of your own Affirmations

_____

_____

_____

_____

_____

_____

_____

_____

_____

_____

_____

_____

_____

_____

_____

_____

_____

_____

_____

_____

_____

_____

_____

_____

_____

_____

_____

_____

_____

_____

_____

_____

_____

_____

_____

_____

RAEVYN SARAI

_____

_____

5

How did I get here?

I thought that if I removed myself from everyone I would avoid drama. I thought if I ignored the sarcastic indirect comments that the problem would go away. It didn't. Things at school had went crazy quick. The girls I once laughed with at lunch and chatted with in our special group chats on Instagram had divided and sides were being taken. Me, being the mature person, I decided to stay out of the drama and remove myself completely.

I watched my sister get into plenty of physical and verbal fights. The fight life was not for me. I had other things to deal with like being depressed.

Besides, I was afraid if I got into a physical fight I would end up killing someone. I had thoughts in my mind that I never told anyone about. They were bad thoughts. Ungodly thoughts. I was a Christian and I loved God, so murder was not supposed to be on my mind, but it was. I wanted to hurt the people that hurt me. I wanted death to be their portion. I would pray for the thoughts to go away. They would for a while, but then they would come right back.

There was a time that something bad had happened at my house. My mother was helping out a family member, like always. The person had done something bad and the cops came busting down our door looking for him and a gun that was used in a shooting. He wasn't there. He hadn't been for months. My mom was at work and I was scared to death! I didn't feel safe so I called my dad to tell him what was going on. When I called him his girlfriend answered, I asked for my dad and she hung up in my ear. I couldn't believe it. So I called back again and she hung up again then the calls went to voicemail. I wanted to cry but I wasn't the crying type. I told my mom what happened and she snapped. She called my mom-mom and told her what happened. Of course, when she was confronted about it, she lied about it. That was a time I really needed my father. If I could drive...I would have gone down there and let's just say black dresses would soon be needed.

Those thoughts scared me because that is not the person I am. When I told my mom how I felt she told me I needed to pray, because those thoughts were evil.

Kimmie said, "I told you she was crazy." Responses like that is why I kept my thoughts to myself. two weeks later in math class, Anna and I were sitting next to each other. Remember I said that we had pretty much split up. The night before she put my picture up on social media and put a TBH-To Be Honest quote saying I was a dyke and I was looking for a girlfriend. I was furious. So, I put her picture up and said she smelled like cat piss!

Everyone found it hilarious because she really did smell like cat piss. The next day during math she hit me with her binder. I told her to stop, she did it again this time harder. I moved my seat and she followed me and tried to hit me again. So this this time. I took the math book and repeatedly smacked her in the head with it. We were sent to the office. That was my first time ever getting in trouble. I lost my self-control.

Since this was my first time getting sent to the office. I was let go with a warning. They did however change our classes.

The Instagram beef continued. Anna involved more people including this real big girl name Keisha, now Keisha was like fifteen years old, in the 8th grade. She was tall like my sister but she was wide. There was nothing I could do with her physically.

The next morning when it was time to go to school. I took my time moving really slowly. My mom was in a bad mood because she got a letter saying I had missed fifteen days from school and Kimmie had gotten suspended for fighting. The month before, the school district sent her a letter threatening her with truancy, so she drove me to school daily which meant she had to alter her work schedule.

I was in the bathroom sitting on the toilet lid with the water running for twenty minutes. My mom banged on the door, "AVA! COME ON I'M GOING TO BE LATE FOR WORK!"

I heard her, but I continued to sit on the toilet with my pajamas on. Five minutes later, I noticed the knob turning on the door. She was breaking in the bathroom! I jumped up and started to brush my teeth. The look on her face when she saw me still in my pajamas was horrifying.

"Are you freaking (she said the real word) serious! Are you trying to make me lose my job!

You know I can't be late. Why Ava! Why are you doing this to me? I swear to God I'm sending you to your dad. I'm not dealing with this!"

Now this was new, she never threatened to send me to my Dad. My grandparents yeah, Dad...never!

"You and your sister are driving me crazy! I do everything for you!" she went ranting and raving then the tears came. I should have known what was next.

Kimmie came into the bedroom half asleep, but not too sleep that she couldn't add in her two cents, "Ava, come on dawg! You're being weird! Just go to school. Don't nobody want to hear her go off first thing in the morning?"

I came out the bathroom and sat on my bed. It was like the entire world stopped.

SMACK! "Really! You gonna sit there and not get dressed?"

SMACK...SMACK...SMACK!

I couldn't respond. I had shut down.

My mom was laying hands on me and not in the biblical way. I NEVER got spankings. There was no need too because I was a good child. I didn't get into fights, I was always on honor roll, I didn't talk back...and I didn't CRY!

I didn't show any emotion at all. My mom was going off like a wild woman, Kimmie had to pull her off me. Kimmie yelled, "Cry! Just cry and she'll stop! You act like you don't care!" The truth was I wasn't acting... I didn't care.

Needless to say I didn't go to school but she did go to work and took my iPhone with her. She forgot I had a laptop…

A Moment to Relate

Some people get triggered easily. As you can see both, Ava and her mother lost their self-control.

My real-life sister has an issue with self-control. The smallest thing can happen and she will flip out. I believe that the brain is triggered rapidly sometimes and it reacts before it can process what is really happening.

Then there are some people who act out because that's what they are known for. If they took the time to think things through before reacting, people would think something is wrong with them, because they are so use to them snapping.

I also believe that people pick on others just to get a reaction out of them. Now to me that's bullying. If you know something bothers someone…why do it? To see their reaction? To be entertained by their misery? Sad.

Think about a time you lost control. What triggered it? What could you have done differently?

_____

_____

_____

_____

_____

_____

_____

_____

_____

_____

List things you can to do to stay in control.

- _____

- _____

- _____

- _____

6

Back to school...

Three days later I returned to school. I didn't give my mother a hard time. I had a plan. I was tired of being bullied. I was tired of being misunderstood. I was tired of being called weird.

I went into the building and the first person I saw was Keisha. She rammed her shoulder into me hard sending me into the lockers. I fell and hit my head. The principal saw what happened and called us into the office. He asked what was going on but I didn't say anything. I asked him if I could go to the bathroom.

Once inside I pulled out the sleeping pills that the doctor had prescribed me and took them all.

I walked to the nurse's office thinking about how I would no longer be a problem for my mother, or the weird little sister, the unwanted daughter or the girl who hated herself. I would no longer exist and their problems would be solved.

Once inside the nurse's office, I told her, "I'm going to kill myself." She pulled me to the side. "What do you mean Ava, do you have a plan?"

I told her, "Yes. I already did it." I showed her the pill bottle…

My Truth...

My ending was more like my beginning. The day my mother went off on me, she didn't go to work as usual. She couldn't because I walked out of the house. I was wearing my pajamas, barefoot with toothpaste running down my mouth.

I didn't care. My fist was balled up because I was angry! I was ready to fight! No one understood what I was going through! I didn't hate school...I hated people! Ignorant, judgmental people who made you feel awkward because you didn't fit in with their crowd. Because I didn't talk like them, I didn't dress like them or wear my hair in certain styles.

I didn't care to have Jordan's or any other name brand sneaker that my mother insisted on me having. I liked Sketcher Twinkle Toes. I liked wearing hoodies and tights. I didn't want to wear form fitting dresses revealing my shape. I wasn't interested in the type of attention it would bring. Because I didn't dress like the typical girl didn't mean I was a dyke, lesbian or tom boy. I was Raevyn and that obviously wasn't enough.

Unlike Ava, I was 11 years old when I decided I was going to take my life. My mother switched me to a Charter school that catered to my "culture". She thought that I would benefit from it- All because I had made a comment that was taken out of context. I said, "I don't deal with *those* types of African Americans." That caused an uproar on both sides of my family. The pictures on my social media didn't help so she decided to put me around more African

Americans, hoping I would appreciate and love myself. The thing was I did love myself!

It wasn't until everyone started to point out my "flaws" that my outlook on myself began to change. Maybe I *was* ugly, *too* dark, or bald headed. Maybe that's why no one took to me like they did Tryniti. Maybe I should act out in school, be disrespectful and fight. Then my mom would be able to spend more time with me. That's the way I was thinking.

When I returned to school and the incident happened with Keisha that was it for me. I didn't use pills like Ava, I went to the nurse's office and I told her I wanted to kill myself.

"She said Raevyn, do you have a plan?" I told her yes, "I had a pair of scissors in my book bag and I was going to stab myself in the neck."

My mother was called immediately and I was admitted into the Rockford Center for inpatient treatment.

My sister was out for blood. She went up to the school ready to fight the entire 8th grade! My mother was devastated…so devastated, I thought she was going to have to admitted to a hospital. I stayed for almost two weeks and I went through two years of outpatient counseling. I would be lying if I said that was my last time at Rockford. I went to intense outpatient treatment three times, including earlier this year.

Did it help? Not in the way people thought it would. It was an escape plan for me. Whenever I felt that anxiety was taking over me I would go. I had developed a phobia of being around crowds-but it only occurred when I was in school. I refused to take their medications because deep down I knew there was nothing wrong with me.

No, I wasn't in denial.

I had realized that there was nothing wrong with *me*...ever. I was an exceptional, unique and intelligent young lady. I wasn't meant to be like other people. How did I all of a sudden come to that conclusion? I knew I didn't belong in a mental hospital!

I prayed. I listened to God. I read other people's stories and I learned to love myself!

So, I no longer care if I'm called weird, or odd, because I am. We all are. I believe God made us in his image so we are all great. I could have easily taken the route that Ava took but what good would that have done. I had to live so

I can share this story with other young people who are misunderstood and bullied.

I do want to add this. I know that mental illness is real and I do suffer from anxiety. If your doctor prescribes you medicine… take it. It helps some people. It just wasn't for me.

Don't give up on your parents. Talk to them and help them understand what you are going through. Even if you have a parent that is not active in your life; don't give up on them! Pray that things get better!

I pray for my dad and I love him. I hope one day that we can have a real father and daughter relationship. I do need and love you dad!

I want to leave you with this, LOVE YOURSELF! BE TRUE TO YOURSELF! KEEP GOD FIRST!

XoXo,

Raevyn Sarai